"My name is Myrtle. started when I couldn't make friends because I was too shy."

Hana

Ernie

Ellen

Betty

Owen

FRancis

MYRTLE

Rosie

MYRTLE, THE TURTLE WHO WAS SHY
A RED FOX BOOK 978 1 862 30507 6

First published in Great Britain by Red Fox,
an imprint of Random House Children's Books
A Random House Group Company

This edition published 2008

1 3 5 7 9 10 8 6 4 2

Text © Red Fox 2008
Hana's Helpline © 2006 Calon Limited
Hana's Helpline is a registered trademark of Calon.

Red Fox Books are published by Random House Children's Books,
61–63 Uxbridge Road, London W5 5SA

www.kidsatrandomhouse.co.uk
www.rbooks.co.uk

Addresses for companies within The Random House Group Limited can be found at: www.randomhouse.co.uk/offices.htm

THE RANDOM HOUSE GROUP Limited Reg. No. 954009

A CIP catalogue record for this book is available from the British Library.

Printed in China

MYRTLE

THE TURTLE WHO WAS SHY

It was Myrtle's first day
at her new school.
She was very scared
about going in
without her mum.
"But I don't know
anyone," Myrtle
whispered quietly.
"Everyone is a little
nervous when they
go to a new school.

It'll be fine once you've settled in," said
Myrtle's mum.

Hana and Francis arrived at the
school gate.

"Hello. What's your name?" Hana
asked Myrtle.

Myrtle ducked down into her shell
and hid.

"She's a little bit shy," said Myrtle's mum.

Mrs Winger waited for all the little animals to be quiet. "Right, children," she said. "We have a new pupil today. Her name is Myrtle. Say 'hello' to Myrtle, everyone!"

Everyone turned to look at Myrtle but she was hiding in her shell.

Mrs Winger started to take the register. All the little animals said, "Yes, Miss," but Myrtle was still inside her shell.

"Myrtle," said Mrs Winger, but there was no reply.

"Myrtle," said Mrs Winger loudly.

"Yes, Miss" said Myrtle from inside her shell. Mrs Winger could hardly hear her.

Ernie, Rosie and Francis tried
to make friends with Myrtle.
She really wanted to play
with them but she just
couldn't help going into
her shell every time they
tried to talk to her.

   Myrtle sat on the swing
on her own and wished she
could join the other little
animals on the roundabout. It
wasn't fun always playing on her own.
Maybe it was time to do something about it . . .

Myrtle lay on her bed and started to daydream about what it would be like if she wasn't shy . . .

She walked into school and all the little animals waved and said, "Hi, Myrtle." She waved at them and walked towards her friends.

Ellen, Francis and Rosie rushed towards her.

"Hey, Myrtle, I love your pencil case," said Rosie.

"Thanks," said Myrtle. "Better dash — I've got a birthday party to go to."

Myrtle decided to go and see Hana and see if she could help. Hana listened carefully to Myrtle's problem. "You'd love to be able to make friends, you mean?" she asked. Myrtle nodded.

"I know the perfect solution," said Hana. "Let's play a game of 'Let's Pretend'." She pulled out a puppet and put it on her hand. "Now pretend that you are the big daddy bear. Repeat after me. Who's been eating my porridge?"

Myrtle looked up at Hana and whispered, "Who's been eating my porridge?"

Hana smiled at her and said, "Can you say that a bit louder, poppet?"

Myrtle nodded and said in a gruff bear voice, "Who's been eating my porridge?"

The next day, Myrtle and her mum were at the roundabout with Hana and Francis. "Ready to go on?" said Hana.
  "You'll love it," said Francis. Myrtle looked unsure.
  "Pretend you are the big daddy bear," whispered Hana.
  Myrtle nodded bravely and got onto the roundabout.

At first Myrtle liked the roundabout but then more children got on and started to spin it faster.

"I don't like it, I don't like it," she cried and ran to her mother.

Owen and Betty were practising a puppet show for all the little animals.

"Who's been sitting in my chair?" growled Owen.

"Very good, Owen," said Betty. "You're not nervous now, are you?"

Myrtle looked at Owen. "You get nervous, too?" she asked.

"Sometimes - not very often," said Owen. He held up the puppets. "Who's been eating my . . . oh . . . oh . . ."

Betty looked worried. "Owen's forgotten his lines," she said to Myrtle. "Would you take his place? I heard you earlier and I thought you were really good."

Myrtle looked out at all the children waiting for the puppet show to begin. She nodded at Betty and put the glove puppet on.

Hana introduced the show. "Hello, everybody. Tonight I present our puppet show, 'The Three Bears'."

When the show finished, all the little animals clapped and cheered, and when Myrtle came out and took a bow, they clapped and cheered even more.

"That was brilliant, Myrtle," called Ellen. "Three cheers for Myrtle, everyone."

Everyone cheered, "Hip, hip, hooray! Hip, hip, hooray! Hip, hip, hooray!" Myrtle had lots of friends after that and she didn't feel so shy any more.

Hana's Help Point

Hana's tips if you are feeling a bit shy

If you are shy and find it hard to make friends, don't worry! Hana can help!

It's OK to be Shy

★ Shy people are often good listeners and nice to be around.

★ Instead of being shy maybe you are just quiet!

★ Some people are noisy and some people are quiet. It's good to have variety!

Making Friends

★ It's easier to make friends who like the same things as you.

★ Asking questions is a good way to get to know someone.

★ Say something nice to someone.

★ Smile! People will smile back – this is a good way to make friends.

Get Involved

★ Invite people round.

★ Activities that can be done in a group are a good way to make friends. You could take up a musical instrument or play some sport.

★ Joining in can be fun and is better than watching from the side!

DON'T FORGET TO SMILE!!

"So remember . . .

. . . if you're in trouble and you need help,
ring me, Hana, on **Moo, Baa,
Double Quack, Double Quack!**"